A book about sharing and caring for the environment –
for Leon, who does.

Tropical rainforests cover just 2% of the world's land surface but contain over half of the earth's wildlife! Rainforests also clean our atmosphere, prevent climate change and recycle huge quantities of water that feed the rivers, lakes and oceans. With less rainforest, droughts would be more common, leading to famine and disease. More than 25% of our modern medicines originate from tropical forest plants! But what we've already discovered is just the tip of the iceberg.

Even though the earth depends on the rainforests in these ways, we are still removing forests from the planet at a faster pace than they can grow back. Much of the world's rainforest has been destroyed for road building, new towns, agriculture, logging, mining and oil. Sadly, extinction of species through habitat loss has never been greater.

Rainforest Concern was established to protect threatened natural habitats, the biodiversity they contain and the indigenous people who still depend on them for their survival. To find out more about the work that we do, or to adopt your very own acre of rainforest, go to www.rainforestconcern.org

SIMON AND SCHUSTER
First published in Great Britain in 2009 by Simon and Schuster UK Ltd
1st Floor, 222 Gray's Inn Road, London WC1X 8HB

Text and illustrations copyright © 2009 Charles Fuge
The right of Charles Fuge to be identified as the author and illustrator of this work
has been asserted by him in accordance with the Copyright, Designs and Patents Act, 1988
All rights reserved, including the right of reproduction in whole or in part in any form
A CIP catalogue record for this book is available from the British Library upon request

ISBN: 978 1 41691 036 7 (HB)
ISBN: 978 1 41691 037 4 (PB)

Printed in Singapore
This book is printed on FSC paper

1 3 5 7 9 10 8 6 4 2

THE TERRIBLE GREEDY FOSSIFOO

Charles Fuge

SIMON AND SCHUSTER

London New York Sydney

The creatures of the Great Green Forest LOVED their home. The trees were covered with delicious fruits, the bushes were bursting with juicy berries and everyone lived happily together.

That is until . . .

the terrible greedy Fossifoo arrived!

He had come from far, far away,
crashing over mountains,

flattening grasslands,

stomping through lakes
and rivers . . .

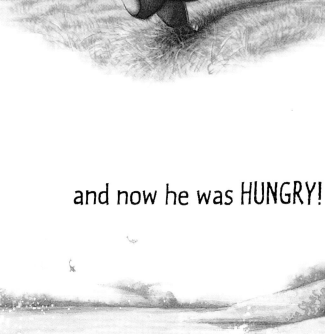

and now he was HUNGRY!

The forest had always provided plenty for **all** the creatures,
but now they could only watch as the greedy Fossifoo
helped himself to everything he could find.

Soon there was nothing left to eat in the whole forest
but the Fossifoo was **so** greedy that **still** he wanted more . . .
and now he was ANGRY!

"Watch this!" he roared and he tore a tree right out
of the ground.

This made the Fossifoo feel MUCH better.
So he tore up another . . .

        and another . . .

                and another!

"Aren't I big?" he bellowed.
But nobody heard – everyone had run away!

Soon the Fossifoo had torn up every last
tree in the forest . . . and now he was HOT!

"Watch this!" he boomed and, to cool down, he
jumped right into the lake with a gigantic SPLASH . . .
and emptied it!
"Aren't I clever?" he bellowed.
But nobody heard – all the fish had disappeared!

By this time, the Fossifoo had bashed, crashed,
munched and splashed . . . and now he was THIRSTY!

"Watch this!" he yelled. Then he reached up into the sky, grabbed a raincloud and wrang it out – right into his enormous mouth. Then he emptied all the other clouds – just for fun!

"Aren't I . . ."
The Fossifoo spun around to see who was watching.

Nobody was!

The Fossifoo looked around — nothing moved.

The Fossifoo listened — not a sound.

The Fossifoo waited for an hour, then a day, then a week.

A year passed by and the forest was completely dry and bare.

Still nobody came.

"What have I done?" whispered the
Fossifoo, and he started to cry.

He cried and cried and cried until he had no tears left to cry. If only he had taken care of the beautiful forest.

Then he noticed it — beneath his feet, watered by all the tears, a tiny seed had sprouted.

The Fossifoo knew that the seed would need more water if it was to grow big and strong — but there was not a single drop left in the forest.

So the Fossifoo leapt up and raced to the Faraway Mountains where he carefully gathered clouds from the mountain tops and hurried them back to where the forest once stood.

There he gave each cloud a gentle squeeze and out poured the rain! One by one, other seeds hidden in the dry earth began to sprout.

Cared for by the Fossifoo, some seeds grew into tall trees and began to bear fruit, others blossomed into bushes bursting with berries.

By now the Fossifoo was VERY hungry, but this time he didn't guzzle ALL the fruit and berries. This time, he took just enough to fill his empty belly.

The rest he either planted in the ground or left to ripen on the trees and bushes.

Before long, rainwater filled the lake and the Great Green Forest was beautiful once more.

There was just one thing missing – the forest creatures!
The Fossifoo would have to get them back!

So he filled his arms with fruit and set off to find them. He trod **gently** over mountains

softly through grasslands,

and **carefully** across lakes and rivers.

Everywhere he went, he told the creatures that he found how lovely the forest had become. He tempted them with his tasty treats and he promised never to stomp, or bash, or crash ever again!

One by one they followed the Fossifoo home . . .

and now he was HAPPY!

From that day on, no creature in the Great Green Forest went without food or shelter again. Everyone lived happily together as the Fossifoo watched over their beautiful home, making absolutely sure that everything was shared equally – and who would argue with a terrible, not-so-greedy Fossifoo?!